CLASSIC FAIRY TALES

Cinderella

Retold by Adèle Geras

Illustrated by Gwen Tourret

MACDONALD YOUNG BOOKS

First published in Great Britain in 1996
by Macdonald Young Books
61 Western Road
Hove
East Sussex BN3 1JD

Designed by Shireen Nathoo Design

Typeset in 20pt Minion
Printed and bound in Belgium by Proost International Book Co.

British Library Cataloguing in Publication Data available.

ISBN: 0 7500 1994 8
ISBN: 0 7500 1995 6 (pb)

Once, long ago, a certain baron took as his second wife a widow who had two daughters of her own. Their names were Araminta and Zenobia. The baron's own daughter longed for the love of her new sisters, and looked forward to the care of her new mother, but Araminta and Zenobia were vain and haughty, and the baroness was unkind.

"Come," they called, "and brush our hair and fold our clothes and turn down our beds."

"And sweep the cinders away from the hearth," added the cruel baroness, "and your reward will be a new name: Cinderella."

Cinderella swept the hearth. She polished the silver. She washed and ironed the clothes that Araminta and Zenobia threw on the floor at night. Although she wept in her heart, she said nothing to her father, for she did not wish to distress him.

But the baron fell ill and died. When she was alone, Cinderella shed her tears at last, for she knew that there was no one in the world now who truly loved her.

But winter turned to spring and spring turned to summer, and one day a footman from the palace arrived at the door. He handed the baroness a fine, white envelope, sealed with the royal seal.

"Look, daughters!" said the baroness, "Prince Angelo is seeking a wife... there is to

be a Ball. Oh, what joy! What opportunities for you to shine, my precious plums!"

"Am I invited to the ball?" Cinderella whispered.

"Most certainly not," said Araminta.

"It's fortunate that the prince has overlooked you," said Zenobia, "for your clothes are hardly suitable."

"Still," said the baroness, "there's no reason why you shouldn't help us prepare for the occasion."

Cinderella spent the next two days laundering and stitching, polishing and pressing, draping and brushing, bathing and perfuming, oiling and powdering, rouging and crimping and at last Araminta and Zenobia were satisfied that the prince would certainly choose one of them for his bride.

The carriage came to the door, and the baroness and her daughters left for the palace.

"Have warm drinks ready for our return," Zenobia called out as they drove off.

Cinderella sat on her stool beside the fire and stared into the flames.

"There will be music and dancing in the palace," thought Cinderella.

"And would it please you to dance?" someone said.

Cinderella jumped up, startled, and there, standing in a shadowy corner was a lady dressed in a gown of shimmering white.

"Who are you?" Cinderella asked.

"I am one who wishes you well," said the

lady. "You may call me Godmother, and I shall bring you the best of my gifts."

"You are kind," Cinderella sighed, "but I fear no one can help me. The music will be playing at Prince Angelo's ball, but I am sitting here weeping when I long to be there dancing."

"It is not too late. You shall go to the ball," said the lady. "Go to the garden and fetch these things: a pumpkin, four white mice, two lizards, and a big black rat."

"How will I find them?" Cinderella cried. "I have never seen such creatures in our garden."

"All that is needful will be there," came the answer.

When the lady stepped into the garden,
Cinderella was waiting on the terrace.

"I see that you have found everything,"
said the lady, and she took a glowing wand
from the folds of her skirts and touched the
pumpkin. It turned at once into a golden

coach with padded seats covered in scarlet satin and wheels studded with gemstones. The mice became four high-stepping white horses; the lizards stretched into footmen, and the rat grew into a coachman in a velvet coat.

"Now," said the lady, "you may go to the ball."

"You have worked some wondrous enchantment," said Cinderella "and I do not understand it, but I cannot go to the palace in my kitchen dress."

"Ah, yes," said the lady. "The dress... "

She touched Cinderella on the shoulder
with the wand. Her ragged garments melted
into a gown woven of moonlight lace and

satin ribbons, its billowing skirt scattered with thousands of tiny pearls. Cinderella's hair arranged itself into a waterfall of curls, and her old shoes became dainty slippers of cut glass which caught the light and twinkled like diamonds.

"Go now," said the lady, "but be sure to leave the dancing before the clock strikes twelve, for at the stroke of midnight, your glory will vanish and all will return to what it was." Cinderella stepped into the coach.

"Thank you, kind lady," she said. "I will return in good time."

The four white horses pawed the ground, and the golden coach made its way to the palace.

At the ball, Araminta and Zenobia were feeling peevish and disappointed.

"Prince Angelo has not danced with us," sulked Araminta.

"Prince Angelo has not even looked at us," Zenobia said, "but he is looking at someone now. Who can it be?"

18

Cinderella made her way through the magnificent ballroom.

"I am sure," said Araminta, "that I have seen her somewhere before."

"Sssh!" said Zenobia. "Look at Prince Angelo. He is bewitched. He's asking her to dance. Imagine! He's dancing with someone we don't even know!"

"She must be a princess," whispered the courtiers, "from a far country."

Prince Angelo danced with the unknown princess.

"I wish," he said "that we could dance together forever." Cinderella and Prince Angelo danced and danced as if in a dream, and all the courtiers watched them.

"He has eyes only for her," the ladies whispered behind their fans. "He has danced with no one else."

Then the palace clock began to strike. Cinderella whispered:

"Is it midnight?"

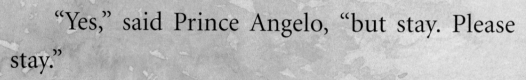

"Yes," said Prince Angelo, "but stay. Please stay."

"I cannot," Cinderella cried. She tore herself out of the prince's arms and ran from the ballroom. She fled through the corridors.

The chimes of the palace clock followed her. She ran so quickly down the marble steps that one of her glass slippers fell off and lay there glittering in the moonlight. As she came to the gate, the stroke of midnight sounded in her ears.

"Now I am Cinderella again," she thought, "but I still have one glass slipper." She took it off and put it in her apron pocket. A yellow pumpkin lying on the grass was all that was left of her splendour, and she began to walk home through the darkness.

Prince Angelo was distraught. He asked everyone whether they had seen the unknown princess. One footman remembered a servant girl beside the gate, but that was all. Prince Angelo frowned.

"I have found one of her glass slippers," he said, "and I shall search the kingdom until I find her."

The next morning, Cinderella said to her stepsisters:

"Will you tell me about the ball?" and Araminta said:

"When you have filled our baths and buttered our toast, perhaps we will tell you. The prince's footman is coming today. There was an unknown princess at the ball last night. The prince has said that he will marry anyone whose foot fits the glass slipper she left behind. I have very elegant, narrow feet, so it will probably be me."

As she spoke, the prince's footman knocked at the door.

"We were expecting you," said the baroness. "These are my beautiful daughters, Araminta and Zenobia. That slipper looks exactly the right size for one of them."

Araminta pushed her foot as far as she could into the slipper, but still her heel hung out at the back.

"My ankles are a little swollen this

morning," she said, "from all the dancing last night."

When Zenobia had her turn, even the tips of her toes would not fit.

"Perhaps if I tried dusting them with talcum powder," she said, "that might help."

"I don't think so," said the footman. "But I should like to try the slipper on this young lady here."

"Quite unnecessary," said the baroness. "Cinderella is not the sort of person in whom the prince would be interested."

"Nevertheless," said the footman, "I have my orders, and they are to try this shoe on every young lady in the land."

He knelt in front of Cinderella, and she slipped her foot easily into the glittering slipper.

"Impossible!" said the baroness.

"Unheard of!" said Araminta.

"Disgraceful!" said Zenobia.

"A perfect fit!" said the footman.

Cinderella took the matching slipper from her apron pocket.

"This," she said, "is what I wore last night to the ball."

"Then you are the love of Prince Angelo's heart," said the footman, "and you must come with me to the palace."

No one in the kingdom could remember an occasion as grand as the wedding of Prince Angelo and Cinderella. The Lady in White stood among the guests and waved her enchanted wand over the bride and groom. Araminta and Zenobia begged for forgiveness, and Cinderella forgave them because she was as kind as she was beautiful. She found them suitable husbands from among the courtiers and with that they had to be content. The baroness boasted to everyone that she had been the best of stepmothers, but of course, no one really believed her.

Garlands of roses were hung in every room in the palace to welcome Prince Angelo and his bride after their wedding, and celebrations in the kingdom continued for a whole week.

Prince Angelo and Cinderella loved one
another deeply and lived together joyfully
until the end of their days.

Other titles available in the Classic Fairy Tales series: